the Zabbit

Leslie
"The Magic's in You!"
Take Care
Jim

To Leslie,
"All of your dreams
Can Someday come true
Just believe in the magic
That's inside of you!"
Best Wishes,
Jim
Jim Walkow
3-9-02

Jim Walkow

Illustrated by Shawn Carson

To Ryan and Kevin, my wonderful sons, with deep love and respect—"The magic's in you."

To John Dalton, CEO and dream maker of Company @ Cloud 9, who believes in the vision, the journey and making a difference.

—From the heart,
Jim

Cloud 9 Publishing, L. L. C.

9545 Katy Freeway, Suite 350

Houston, Texas 77024

(713) 722-8277

www.cloud9publishing.com

www.zabbit.com

The illustrations are rendered in oil paint on canvas.

Printed in China by Palace Press International / Sabra Chili

1 2 3 4 5 6 7 8 9 0

ISBN 0-9710394-0-2

In the beautiful, magical forest of Zimm,
near the banks of the river Ribble Dimm Dimm,
there once was a rabbit...
Abbott the Rabbit.

Now, Abbott the rabbit looked like no other—
not his father, or mother, or sister, or brother.
How he got this way, nobody knows.
He had stripes from his head to the tips of his toes.

Every year he grew bigger;
his stripes, they would grow.

And, everyone laughed
wherever he'd go.

"Your stripes are not right;
they zig and they zag."
"They're fat."
"They are skinny."
"Your stripes even sag."

"Your ears are not straight;
in the middle they drop."
"Your posture is awful
whenever you hop."

"You tumble and stumble before you go plop."
"We're afraid, as a rabbit, you are a FLOP!"

Abbott felt sad from the words he'd just heard,
because others had said what he was...was absurd.

He questioned his parents at bedtime that night.
"Why am I so different? Will things ever be right?
Will the dreams I am dreaming ever come true?"
"The answers," they said, "are all inside you.

You come from a family of master magicians.
Believe in yourself. Carry on our traditions.
What makes you so special are the thoughts in your mind.
You have a purpose in life. Look inside and you'll find
that you can be anything you want to be.
You can control your own destiny.

Keep the love in your heart and always be kind.
Create your own luck by using your mind.
Be brave and courageous and always pursue
whatever you want. You can make it come true.

Do what you love and love what you do,
and you will unlock the magic in you."

The next morning, Abbott awakened to hear
strange noises, loud voices. Up went his ears!
"The Hunter is here!" "No! The Hunter is there!"
"Run for your life. Run and take care!"

Abbott ran from the Hunter...
he ran far away...
straight into a trap
that very same day.

When the Hunter arrived, he asked,
"What have we got?
You look like a rabbit,
but what if you're not?
I'm hungry and dinner
is long overdue.
My stomach is growling.
I want RABBIT STEW!"

Abbott had never felt this kind of fear...
never, ever in his rabbit career.
He could no longer hide.
He could not run away.
There was no one to turn to,
except himself, on this day.

His life flashed before him...all that he knew,
all he was taught, and—if caught—what to do.
hen Abbott remembered what his parents had said
every night, just before they tucked him in bed.
"Keep the love in your heart and always be kind.
Create your own luck by using your mind."

He became quite inspired, for he now realized
that knowledge is power when problems arise.
"I'll use what I've learned to get out of this trouble."
And, he magically turned himself into a double.

Two rabbits with stripes soon became four.
They doubled, then tripled to become 24.

Then they all disappeared to be one, like before.
"Amazing," said the Hunter, "I want to see more!"

Abbott then threw his stripes in the air.
Soon rainbows encircled the clouds everywhere.
Clouds were gift-wrapped in bright colored bows.
Abbott had staged a spectacular show.
He even invented a new type of RAIN-BOW!

With a wave of his hand,
day turned into night.
Stars and stripes played together—
an incredible sight.

Thunder and lightning
lit up the sky.
Better than fireworks
on the Fourth of July.

The Hunter exclaimed, "You're really quite rare.
Can you give me good luck? Pull it out of thin air?
If you can, little rabbit, your life I will spare.
Who are you? What are you?
A magical hare?"

"Magic?" asked Abbott. "Magic, you say?
Perhaps I am magical, in a way.
I have stripes like a zebra.
I look like a rabbit.
I can bring you good luck,
for I am a ZABBIT!

Now, would you rather have luck,
or dinner for two?
Be happy forever,
or have Zabbit stew?
The illusion of magic
is all that you see.
The luck that you want
is inside of you...
it's inside of me.
For you can be anything
you want to be.
How would you like to
change places with me?

You could see what it's
like to be caught in a trap...

or pulled by your ears out of a hat.
Do you think it is right
to be treated like that?

Every day of your life you have choices to make.
You can choose to be angry, to fear and to hate,
or to be loving and kind, and good luck you'll create

You think I am trapped?
It's really not true.
The one who is trapped...
perhaps it is you.
Are you really and truly
one of a kind?
A smart human being
who uses his mind?
Or, are you trapped
by your thoughts
that are sometimes unkind?
The choice is yours.
It's up to you to do
what you know
is right to do.

You could set an example that forever would stay,
if you're the first hunter to let go of his prey.
Imagine the headlines the papers would say.
What if others should follow what you do today?
The reward is in giving. It's simple but true.
When you give to others, it comes back to you."

"What luck," said the Hunter. "What luck that we met.
You and your words I shall never forget.
If I do what you say—for what you say is correct—
what I do every day could have a lasting effect.
I'll tell all the hunters to leave you alone...
to always be kind to you and your own.

Are you king of the Zabbits?
Do you have your own throne?

Take care lucky Zabbit.
You're free to go home.
Share the 'Luck of the Zabbit'
wherever you roam.

From now to forever
let it be known...
this forest shall be a
NO HUNTING ZONE!"

Well, word got around what happened that day,
and soon rabbits had stripes going every which way.
They wanted to be like the Zabbit they knew.
They hoped his good luck would rub off on them, too.
In fact, Zabbit stripes were in such great demand,
that wherever they turned was a Zabbit paint stand.

ZABBIT PAINT

ZABBIT PAINT

The Zabbit was free. The Hunter was gone.
And, everyone gathered on the Zabbit's front lawn—
a turtle, a duck, a bear, and a frog;
a dove on a deer, and a toad on a log;
an owl, and a skunk,
and a baby chipmunk.
The rabbits arrived
all wearing their stripes.
They believed in the Zabbit
and animal rights.

They remembered they once had made fun of Abbott.
How did he turn into their hero the Zabbit?
When the Zabbit appeared, they all bowed with respect.
"Be our king. You have saved us with your intellect.
Is there somehow your good luck we can collect?"

The Zabbit, he spoke with
great poise and great pride.
All the animals listened,
and none were dry-eyed.
"You, too, are quite special.
We're just different types.
I'm no better than you,
just because I have stripes.

Since we each are quite different,
we must always take care
to cherish what's different
when we find it somewhere.
In ourselves or in others,
it matters not where.
It's what you do
with what you've got.
It's saying I CAN
and never CANNOT!

ABBOTT-TA-ZABBIT,
the magic's in you.
You can do anything
you want to do.
All of your dreams
can someday come true.
Just believe in the magic..
that's inside of YOU!!"